Read•A•Picture

LET'S GO

Library of Congress Cataloging-in-Publication Data

Marks, Burton.
    Let's go / by Burton Marks; illustrated by Paul Harvey.
       p.   cm.—(Read-a-picture)
    Summary: In rhyming text and rebuses, a boy describes how, in his
imagination, different types of transportation can take him to many
marvelous places.
    ISBN 0-8167-2413-X (lib. bdg.)   ISBN 0-8167-2414-8 (pbk.)
    [1. Transportation—Fiction. 2. Imagination—Fiction. 3. Stories
in rhyme. 4. Rebuses.] I. Harvey, Paul, 1926-   Ill. II. Title.
III. Series: Marks, Burton. Read-a-picture.
PZ8.3.M39148Le 1992
[E]—dc20
                                      91-9986

Published by Watermill Press.
Copyright © 1991, 1992 by Joshua Morris Publishing, Inc.
Written by Burton Marks.
Illustrated by Paul Harvey.
All rights reserved.
Printed in Singapore.

10 9 8 7 6 5 4 3 2 1

Read·A·Picture

LET'S GO

By Burton Marks
Illustrated by Paul Harvey

Watermill Press

Z16651 3/94

ON RAINY NIGHTS

On rainy nights when I'm tucked into ,

dreamy thoughts go through my head.

I hear the patter of the ,

and look! My becomes a plane!

It whizzes out the  ,

and soars above the .

I wave to all the passing ,

the , and .

The below looks very small;

I cannot see my at all.

The places where I always play

are tiny from far away.

I journey past the  and

till morning comes and then,

my plane flies back into my room,

and becomes my  again.

FIND-A-PICTURE

Somewhere in this picture are:

a , a , a , a  , and a  . Can you find them?

OFF I GO!

I'm taking a ✈ to Japan,

I'm boarding a 🚂 for Pakistan,

I'm flying a 🚀 up to the 🌙,

and I won't be back any time soon.

I'm riding my 🚲 to Peru,

I'm driving a 🚗 to Timbuktu,

I'm sailing a ⛵ to Bombay,

I must be going—if Mom says it's OK.

MY LITTLE CAR

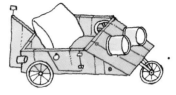

I have a shiny little .

It's ever so much fun.

I never stop to fill it up—

it needs my 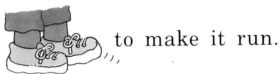 to make it run.

MY "JUST PRETEND" TRAIN

My  is just four kitchen

that line up in a row.

But it can take me anywhere

that I would like to go.

I can cross the highest ,

I can ride down to the sea,

or go deep into the

if that's what pleases me.

I can journey to a

in a land far, far away.

Because my  is "just pretend"

it takes me where I want to play.

PICTURE A RIDDLE

- What has one horn, runs all day, and gives milk?

- What bird can heavy things?

- What did they call the first bus in America?

- What do you call a sleeping bull?

- What has teet but cannot bit

- milk truck
- bulldozer
- Columbus
- crane
- comb

MY BOAT OF WOOD AND NAILS

One day I took some 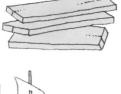 and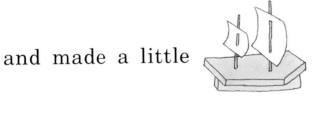

and made a little 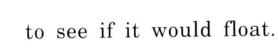 .

I put it in the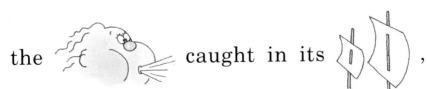

to see if it would float.

It drifted quickly out to sea,

the  caught in its  ,

and I never ever saw it again,

my  of and  .

MY VERY OWN SPACESHIP

I'm building my own spaceship

from things I have on hand—

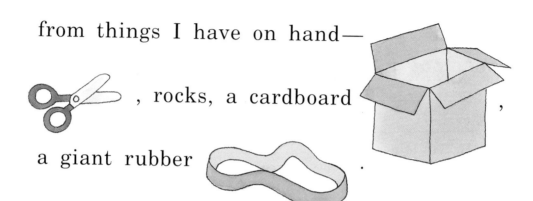 , rocks, a cardboard ,

a giant rubber .

Roller  and paper plates,

mops and  and frying ,

toothpicks, , and ice-cream sticks,

safety  and garbage cans,

zippers, snaps, and bottle ,

 and pails and worn-out ,

strings and  and mattress ,

nuts and bolts and metal .

I've been working since this morning
and I cannot figure why,
when I started up the engine,
my spaceship wouldn't fly!

I've checked and rechecked everything—
I'm not sure what to do.
Do you think perhaps it needs
another bottle COLA or **2**?

LITTLE BEAR'S BIRTHDAY

Little Bear is having a party today.

Look! All the guests are on their way.

Can you name the things
that each one brings?

Presents, presents everywhere.
Happy Birthday, Little Bear!

FIND-A-PICTURE

Somewhere in this picture are:

a ![helicopter], a ![sailboat], a ![motorcycle], a ![tow truck], and a ![fire hydrant]. Can you find them?

THE LONG-LEGGED CRANE

Jane McShane is a long-legged

who flies a jet

when she travels to Spain. Unless, of course,

it happens to ☔. In which case,

you might see her taking a .

BARNEY MULDOON

Barney Muldoon is a clever

who can play the bassoon by the light of the

And sometimes in June, in the late afternoon,

he may play you a tune in his hot-air

We  pe **U** enjoyed your trip through this .

Please come back **4** another look!